INTO THE VOLCANO

A GRAPHIC NOVEL
BY CALDECOTT HONOR ARTIST

Don Wood

THE BLUE SKY PRESS
An Imprint of Scholastic Inc. • New York

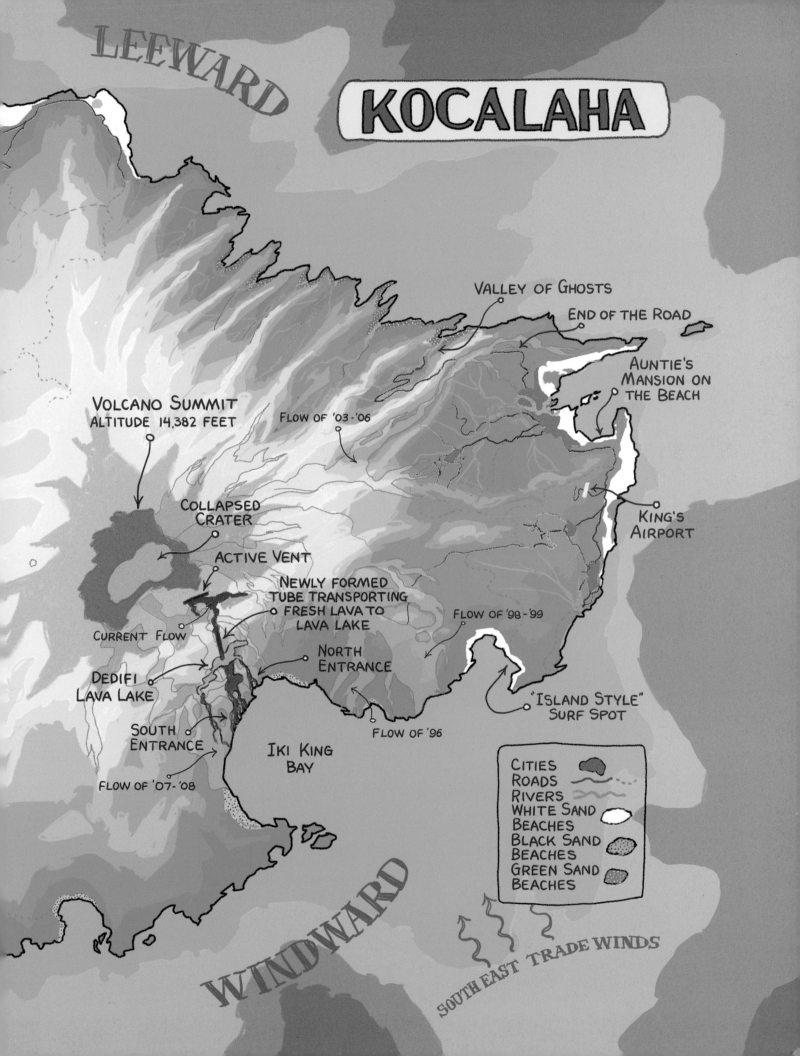

8

26

30

WE ARE RUSHED. I CAN HEAR THE SURF BOOMING. LAVA IS FLOWING FAST.... THIS MAY NOT BE A GOOD IDEA...

...TOO DANGEROUS.

MY SON, YOU OF ALL PEOPLE!

YOU GET OUT THERE AND LEAD OUR FAMILY! DO WHAT MUST BE DONE!

※◎彡☀☒#彡彡! UPHOLD OUR HONOR!

IF THEY GET IT OFF THE ISLAND, IT'S GONE FOREVER.

OK. HEE-YAAAHH! LET'S GO!

KKKRAKK

BUMP
WHUMP

MANGO! PUSH THE BOAT OFF THE ROCKS!

THE STERN LINE, KALEO! THROW IT TO ME!

GOT IT! MANGO! PORT LINE SECURED!?

YO!

KALEO! ANY DAMAGE?!

FORGET IT, KALEO. THIS AIN'T NO FISHIN' TRIP.

IS THAT THE DAWN ALREADY?

NO, THE SUN RISES BEHIND US. THAT'S THE LADY OF THE ISLAND GETTING READY FOR OUR VISIT.

WHAT LADY?

DIDN'T THEY TELL YOU ANYTHING? IT'S THE VOLCANO, KID. IN ABOUT ONE HOUR YOU'RE GOING TO GET QUITE A SHOW. THE LAVA LAKE HAS BREACHED, AND RIVERS OF MOLTEN LAVA ARE FLOWING TOWARD THE SEA.

43

47

48

49

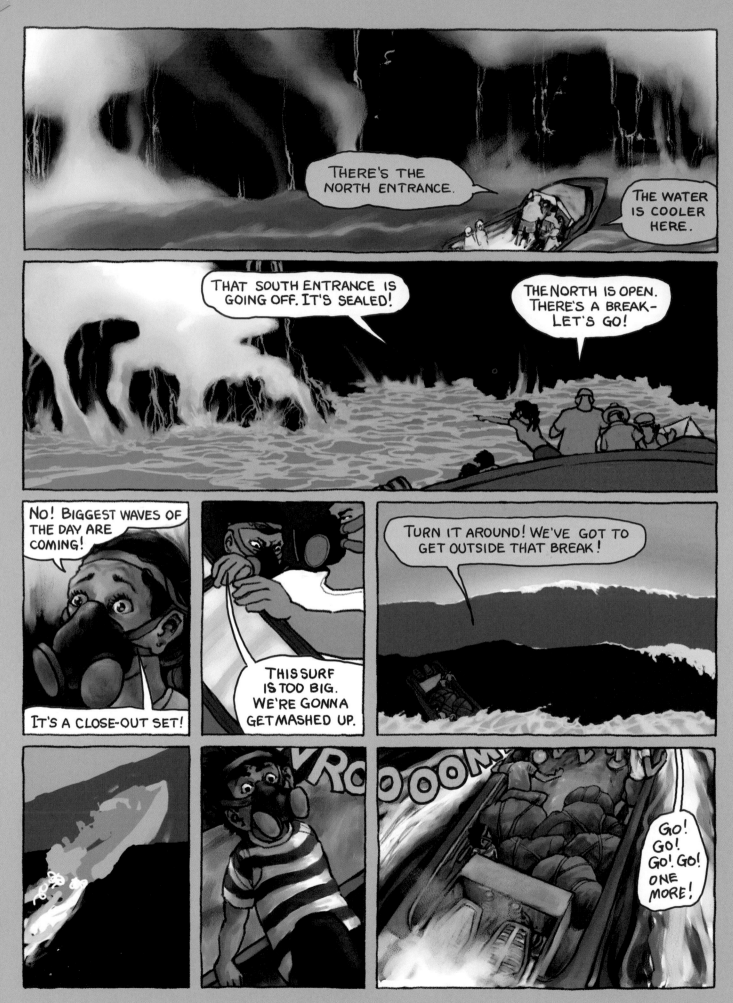

50

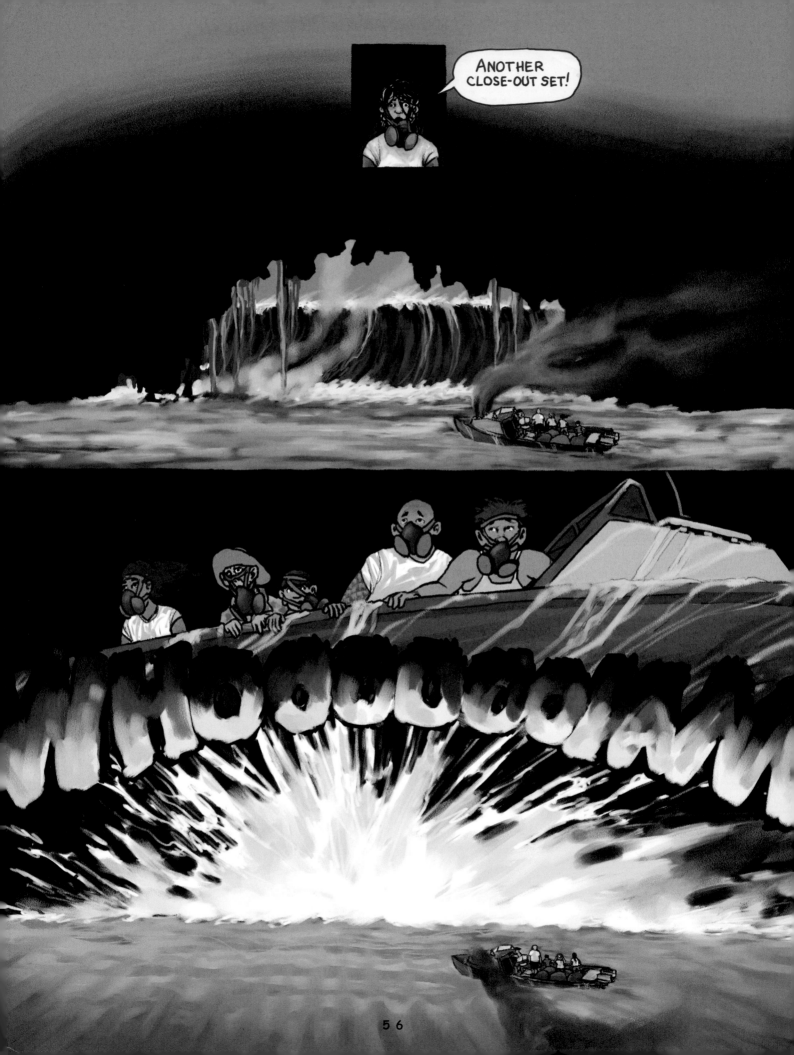

60

70

FROM NOW ON, WE'LL BE ON TACTICAL ALERT.

WHAT'S THAT MEAN?

SOMEONE WILL BE ON WATCH AT ALL TIMES. TONIGHT'S SCHEDULE IS... FIRST WATCH- MANGO, SECOND WATCH- PULINA, I'LL TAKE THIRD WATCH.

WHOA, KID! YOU STARTLED ME!

WHAT ARE YOU WATCHING FOR?

ANYTHING. YOU LOOK LIKE YOU NEED A DRINK WORSE THAN I DO. HAVE A SWIG.

NO, THANKS.

DUFFY! WHERE ARE WE GOING?

C'MON! C'MON!

LOOK!

YOU'VE FOUND YOUR AUNTIE'S CABIN.

SHE STAYED DOWN HERE BEFORE HER HEALTH DETERIORATED. AS YOU CAN SEE FROM ALL THE PHOTOS, SHE IS DEVOTED TO YOUR SIDE OF THE FAMILY.

WHERE'S MY MOTHER?

NOW YOU BOYS RUN ALONG....

GO ON BACK TO WHERE YOU'RE SUPPOSED TO BE, AND LET ME CONTINUE MY SEARCH.

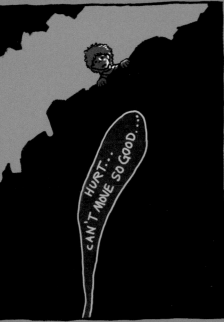

105

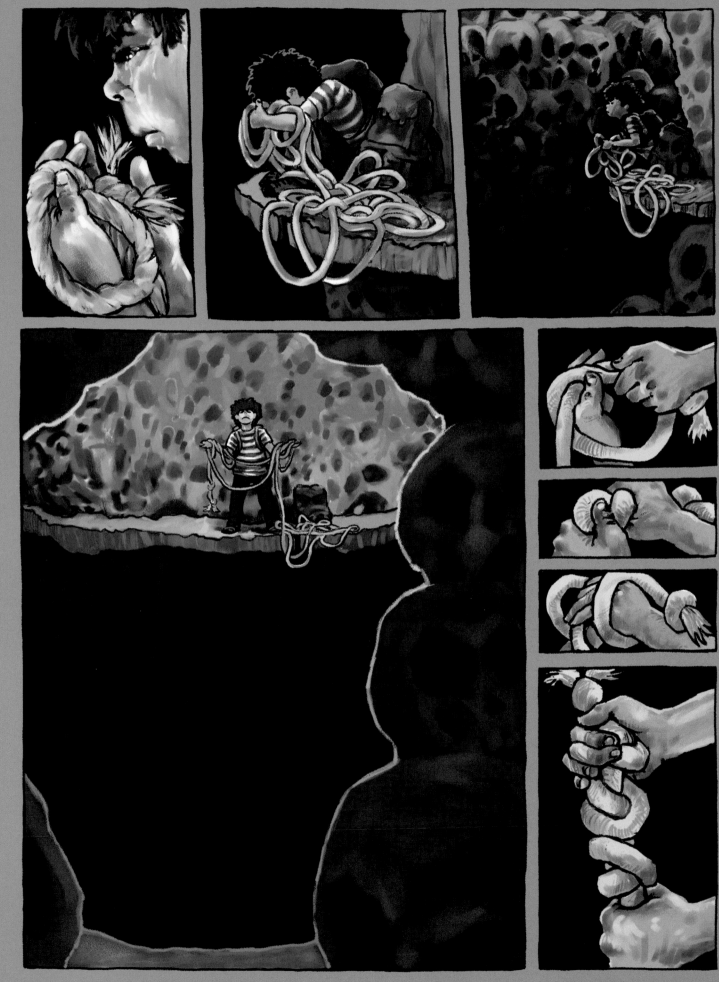

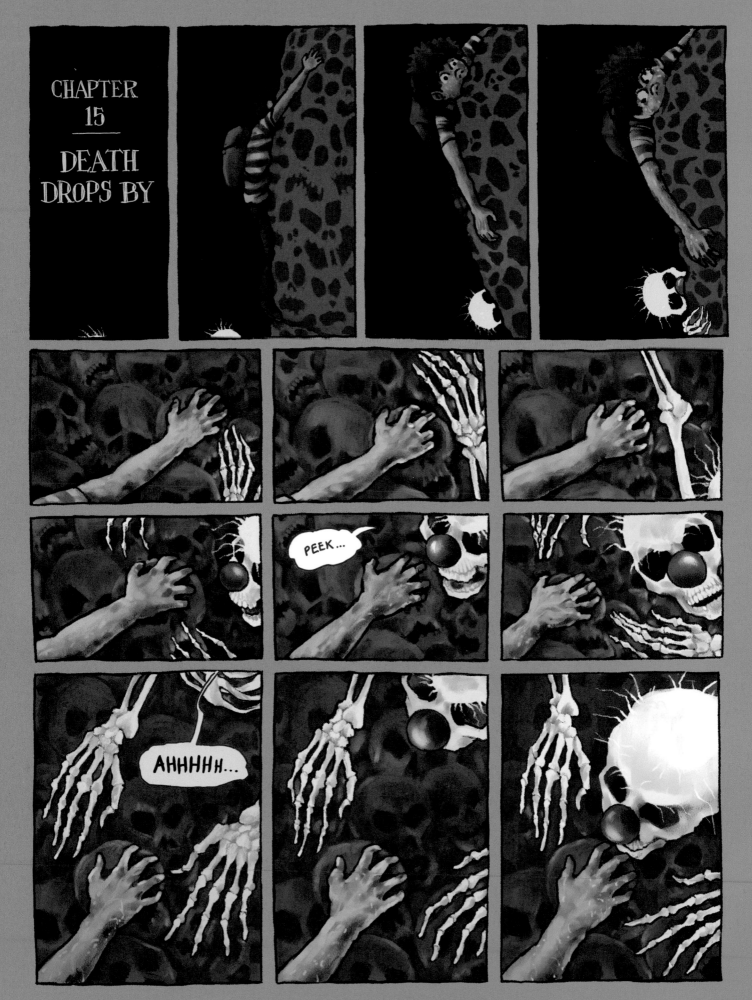

OR MAYBE...HEE-HEEEEEEEE... IT'S THE "FAILURE TO LIVE UP TO YOUR POTENTIAL" THING. YOU COULD HAVE BEEN A GREAT WHATEVER AND CHANGED THE WORLD.

HAW HAW HEE-HEEEEEEE....IF I HAD A NICKEL FOR EVERY TIME I'VE HEARD THAT ONE....

Y'KNOW...

IF YOU HAD FALLEN INTO THIS HOLE...

DUFFY WOULD HAVE RESCUED YOU.

WELL... I SEE THAT YOUR RIGHT LEG IS BEGINNING TO SHAKE.... IT WON'T BE LONG NOW....

SO NOW THAT YOU'VE HAD YOUR LITTLE GESTURE OF DEFIANCE... I'LL JUST SLIDE ON DOWN INTO THE DARK PIT AND WAIT FOR YOU....

♪♫ DUM-DEE-DOO-DEE-DOO... ♫

DOODLE-DEE DAH...

119

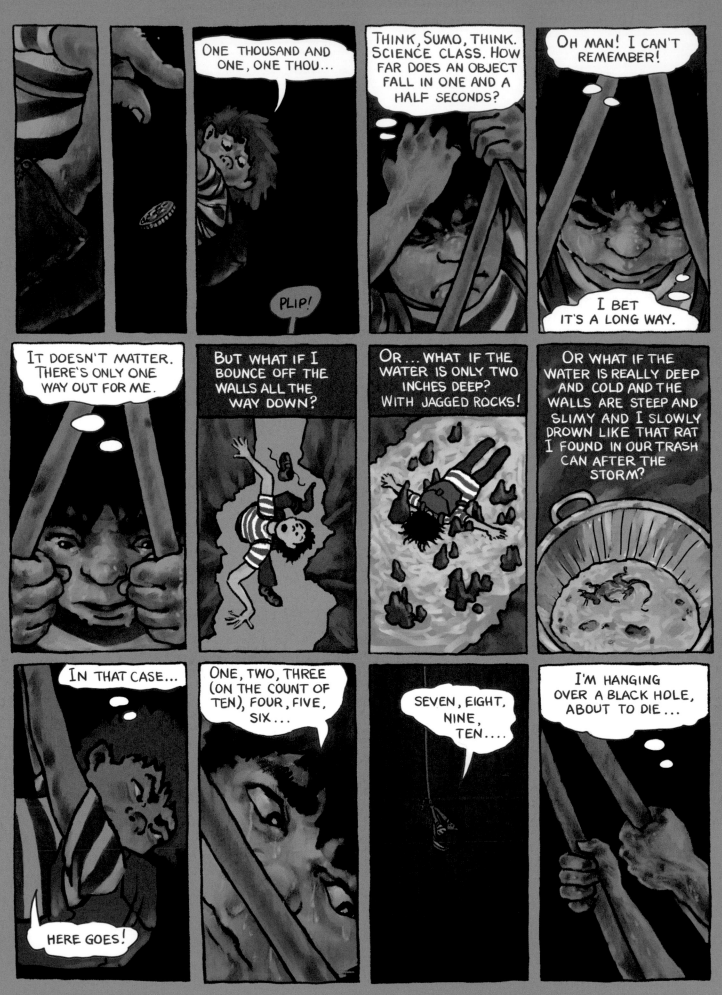

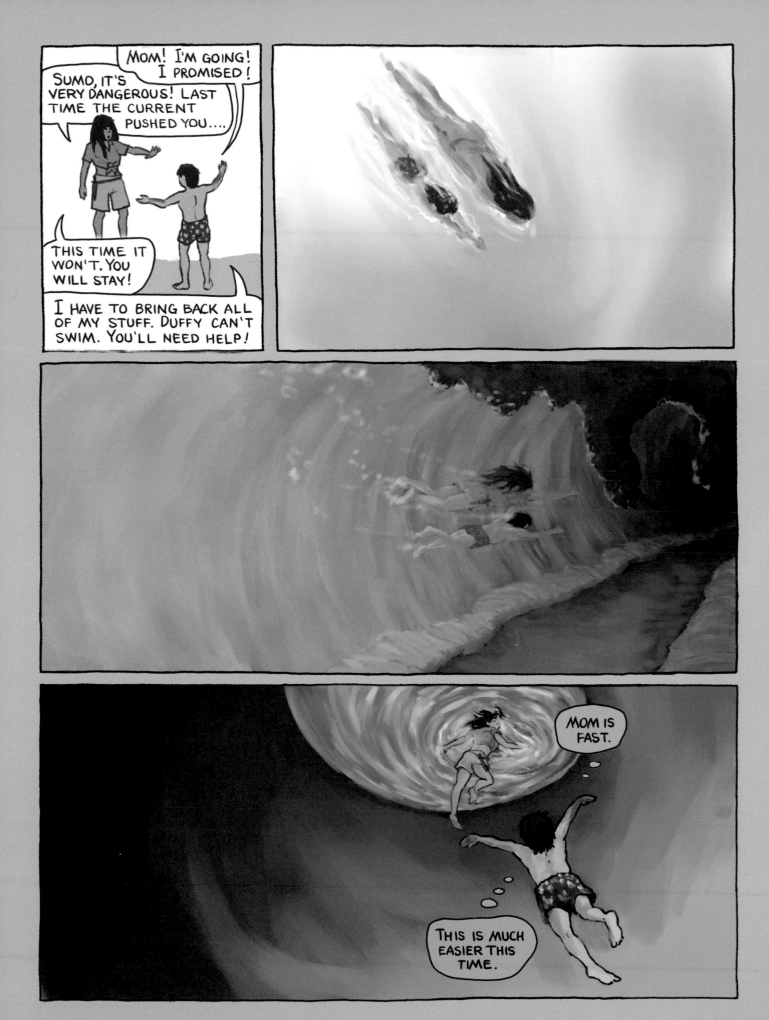

WHMP

IT'S OVER NOW,
BUT THE QUAKES
ARE INCREASING IN
FREQUENCY AND
MAGNITUDE. THIS
TIME WE WERE
LUCKY.

WE SHOULD DROP THE
ENGINES, UNLOAD THE BOAT, AND USE
THOSE TWO OARS TO PADDLE OUT OF HERE.

WOW, SUMO. YOUR
MOM DOESN'T
MESS AROUND.

I CAN'T LEAVE
MY ENGINES.
I MAKE MY LIVING
WITH THESE.

YOU GET US AND OUR STUFF
OUT OF HERE, AND I'LL
BUY YOU NEW ENGINES.

YOU KNOW HOW MUCH
THESE BABIES COST?

ABOUT TWELVE THOUSAND.

LOOK.

150

THIS TIME, NO MISTAKES. THE LAVA FALL IS BIGGER. IF WE HIT A WAVE WRONG, WE'LL BREAK THIS BOAT IN HALF.

IF WE MAKE IT OUT OF HERE, IT'S EIGHT MILES TO THE MARINA. THERE'S A NICE CURRENT TO PUSH US ALONG, SO WE'LL BE SAFE BY DINNER.

I AM DRY.... DOES ANYONE HAVE ANY WATER?

YEAH... I'VE GOT SOME... IN MY PACK.

WELL....

PASS IT AROUND.

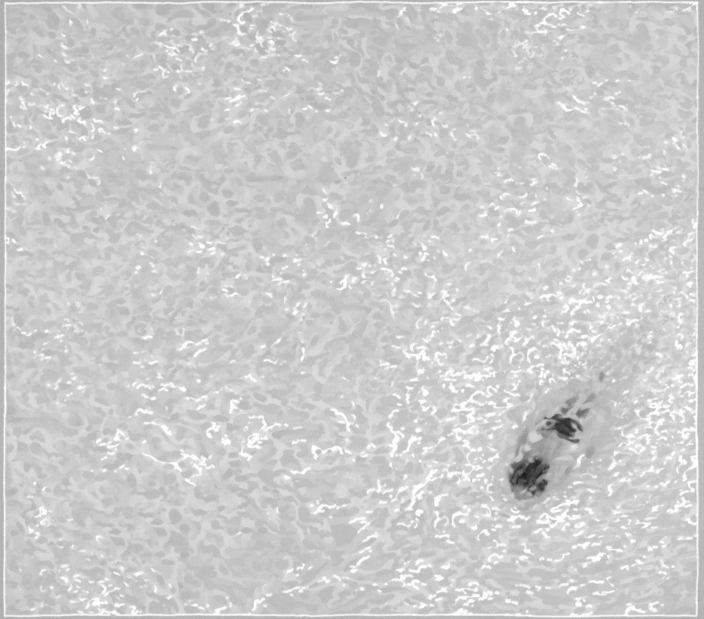

WHAAA!

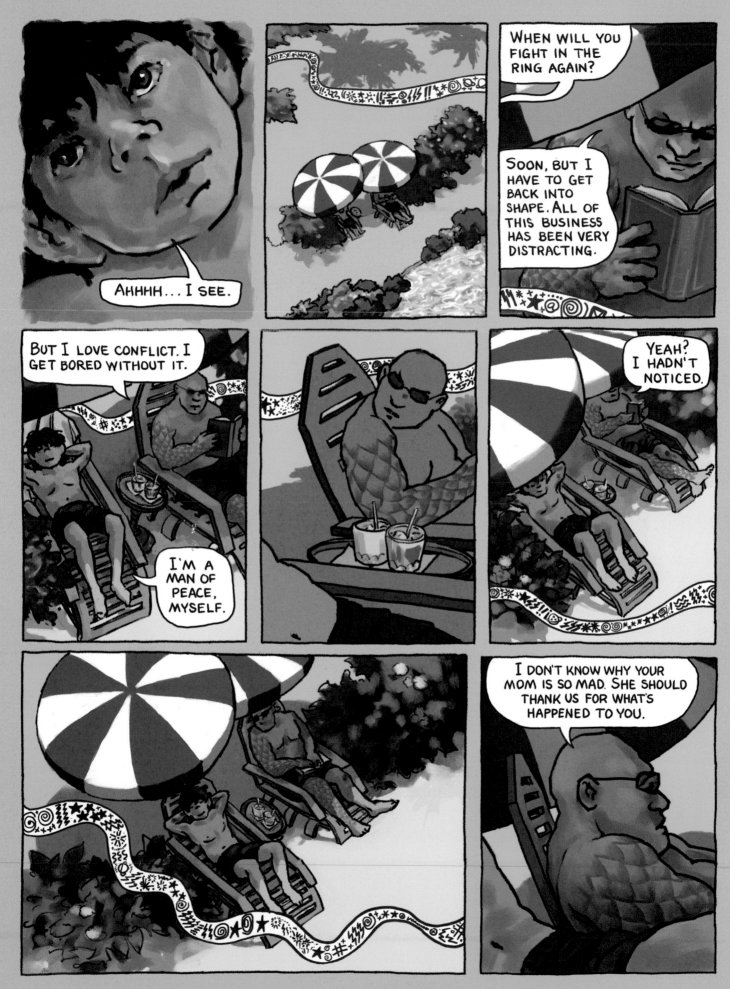

172

THE END

THIS BOOK IS DEDICATED TO AUDREY WOOD.

THE BLUE SKY PRESS

Copyright © 2008 by Don Wood

Library of Congress catalog card number: 2007051084.

ISBN-13 [HC]: 978-0-439-72671-9 / ISBN-10 [HC]: 0-439-72671-9
ISBN-13 [BF]: 978-0-545-10856-0 / ISBN-10 [BF]: 0-545-10856-X

10 9 8 7 6 5 4 3 2   08 09 10 11 12
Printed in Singapore   46
First printing, October 2008